Brooklyn's Song

A novella

Alexis A. Zinkerman

Brooklyn's Song: A novella

To my mom and dad, Rita and Jeff, Robert,
and to Catherine Ryan, who will live in our hearts forever

SCAR TISSUE THAT THEY NEVER SAW

You showed me your scars
that's what best friends do
self-love written all over your arms
I remember
we were at the Lady Gaga concert
at the Allstate Arena when
you said "Wanna see my scars. I'll show you
if you keep it a secret."
You bared your secret shame stoically.
I asked you why
you shook your head
"No need to explain," you said.
Explaining pain seems sort of dumb
"Just don't tell my folks, Brooklyn."
"Please, Brooklyn, don't tell."
"I promise, Emmie."
The concert rocked on
and I wasn't jivin' anymore
I wanted to help
stop your collision course
with disaster.
But
you were already gone.
I could tell by the stare
of your empty eyes, tired,
like you had already given up,
given in.

My dad drove us home
that night to my house
and you stayed up
all night long
making Youtube videos,
senseless angry rants.

We sent you to walk home
alone after plates of morning
coffee, eggs and bacon.

You've disappeared before.
One time the police found you naked
crying in the fountain near the zoo.

This time:
You are gone.
Gone forever.

AFTER YOU'RE GONE

Forever, you cannot see in front
or behind you
Forever, in love or forever in death
So far from Emily's death now
Perchance, to take one'e own life
or to suffer in one's mortal flesh
It's something I'll never understand
Forever, a dirty, cruel world, because
nothing ever lasts that long

I scribble these words in my journal
sitting on the steps of Lincoln Park High School
waiting for the bell to ring. The Chicago air is balmy
for a May day.

The pain of forever
on the other side of light
standing staring at your shadow
in the dark
trembling before purgatory.

My mother once told me after you died
that when someone ends their life they spend
their days in a tortured purgatory, between worlds,
watching how their death affected those that loved them.

We used to laugh together at the girls who were too cool
for us; make clothes together; read each other's zines and
write our own.

I remember the day your mom called my house to say
you wouldn't be around no more; her voice
sharp and pained on our answering machine.
I looked to the floor, then ran to the Fullerton el stop and
silently rode the el for hours dry eyed.

No. I forgot how to cry.
What are you supposed to do, say, move when you
lose your best friend? The newspapers read that you
did the hari kari on the el tracks, you jumped the train
and the train got you.

I got no other friends except for my poetry.

You left me dead inside.
We were blood sisters knew each other
since we were five. Ten years short but I felt like
I knew you all my life.

Remember when we hit the club scene with our fake ids,
jelly bracelets and stiletto heels looking for cute boys.
We met those guys who took us
to that party in the Wicker Park loft.
I tried my first beer. But not you.

You were the good one, on her medication.
You didn't drink.

I got to write a poem for school.
So I think I'll grab a few lyrics from my life:

There were no clues
to your demise
it was a surprise
Or maybe...

We are all to blame
for not listening
to your cry for normalcy
free from meds.

Oh, will I ever be the same
without you?

Was I only given 10 years
to pack in a lifetime of fun?

Now, you leave me alone
and questioning
this life.

I re-copy these lines from my journal onto notebook
paper and tear it off just as the bell rings.

Time for English class
I sit and stare at Mrs. A
Shakespeare's hollow words
ring in my ears
Thoughts blur
I dodge being called on several times
The bell rings again
I hand in my poem

walking past Mrs. A abruptly
hoping she is too busy to notice.

When I'm upset
when I feel bad
when things are incomprehendable,
I like to ride the el through all
the neighborhoods of the city.

I sit sideways in a double seat on the train
my feet on the seat
writing, trying to make sense of what happened
I finger the lace of my Converse
A homeless man wearing an Addidas shirt
asks why I look sad
I don't hear him or
if I did I don't respond.

How do you react in the world
when you feel nothing at all?, when
all your energy has been zapped,
sucked right out of you, when
all you can do is scream senseless
because that is what makes sense
But you don't.
Because it'll look funny, they might come
and lock you up.

They say she was the crazy one
then why is it you who feels insane?

SCREAM inside my head SCREAMSCREAMSCREAM

This is Chicago says the el train.
I get off and climb up the steep steps
to the open air, past the YMCA, past the derelicts
and drunks trying to get sober, trying to believe
in something called hope.

I stopped believing a long time ago,
only to have my belief shattered again
when you left us.
There's a coffee shop on the corner,
one of these trendy Yuppie places,
I order a double espresso and figure
I'll start drinking them to drown the existential exhaust
called my life.

I wander through the bookshops and clothing stores
glimpsing the pretty things
through translucent paper
nothing can get in
at least, nothing good.

I circle the historic Water Tower
round and round
motion feels good
in motion I don't feel.

At dinner, I ease through
the jovial conversation
about the day, listening

to my younger sister
prattle. And excuse
myself when my chicken
is done.

I have studying to do,
algebra test to ace
But studying seems
so pointless.

Northwestern for journalism
seems like a lofty, stupid goal
when you won't be there
studying theatre.

You smiled
as we walked up North Avenue beach
towards the shipwreck deck
Stars lit the sky, cool breeze
shatters silence
This is what you liked
the melodramatic moments
what an actress, you were.

I keep you frozen
this way, immobile,
afraid to move, afraid
I might forget...

FREAKEN' TEACHER

It was just a poem,
a stupid old poem.
Mrs. A told my counselor
I'm insane, she told her
something, if you see something,
say something, the new law of the land.

She misunderstood me,
I knew she would.
Everybody does, except
you, Emily.

My counselor said that if
I wouldn't talk she was
going to call my parents,
as if this would help.

My parents, your parents
don't want to talk about it.

But I think you have to
to get things out,
to break things down,
to understand why.

If it were up to me,
I'd talk about it everyday
except
no one wants to listen.

so I shut up
        silence

That's why I write
in my journal
my secrets reduced
to bad poetry

"Brooklyn, Yoohoo, Brooklyn"
I've been hearing my classmates,
parents, people on the street
call my attention to myself
But I don't care.
Your voices don't matter no more.
They are all hollow.
I am merely a shadow
in Your world.

PSYCHOTHERAPY,
THEY WANNA GIVE ME WHAT?

I sit in front of you
swallowed up by your big couch
averting your wide, questioning eyes
No, you can't know my secrets.
Because I'M NOT CRAZY!

Your office is in a high rise
at North Michigan and Grand
seven floors high
I am to visit you weekly after school
until who knows, how long.

I'll be okay. someday.
Just let me work things out
on my own, i'll be fine.
I can "buck up" by myself.
Resilience, that's the word.

"Is something wrong?" Your kind voice echos.
Kind leads to misunderstanding,
it always does.

"That's all for now. I'll see you next week." you say.
I smile because I told you nothing.

Back at school, Lisa obsequiously wants
to be my friend, she clings to my every move
mundanely chatting about what's hot and what's not

like they do on Entertainment Tonight.
I have a callous way of blowing her off.
But with every blow, she come in closer.
"Let's try out for the school television station."
NO!
You are not my BFF.
Next week already. Oh boy!
I'm in your office again.
Tight-lipped.
"How was your week, Brooklyn?"
Another well-meaning adult
who doesn't, couldn't understand.
A lump forms in my throat,
my eyes burn.

You hand me a box of tissues.
I push it to my side.
Must not cry, trained myself not to cry.
"It's okay if you want to cry, Brooklyn," you say.

"You might be surprised but I know what you are going
through," you say.
You do? This is some type of ploy, open up, then be labeled
crazy.
"When I was around your age, I lost a friend to a car accident."
What am I supposed to say.

I don't allow myself to cry, I say.
"It's okay. I didn't either for a long time," you say.

I think we are getting somewhere...I think...
I think I am going to like Dr. K.

She's safe not like my parents and teachers
I can tell her anything and she doesn't freak or
think I'm a freak.

IN TREATMENT 2 A.M.

Dr. K gives me a card
with her cell phone on it
and it's a real number, the
one she uses for her personal life too.

She tells me to call whenever I need to talk
outside of our Monday sessions,
to call when things get to big, too complicated
in my head to understand.

I don't really call her at 2 a.m., but
I want to. I want to see what she's like
outside of our office sessions, I want to know her as a friend.
But, part of me doesn't want to bother her that late, part of
me knows
I am not life-threatening.
I'm still timid during sessions
afraid to talk, afraid of the power
of my own words.

One day, I bring a small digital camera
with me because afterward I am going
to walk and walk and record
my world in photographs.
I might put some on Facebook or on my blog.
I might not.

You listen
to my
silence.
always letting me know
it is okay to talk or not talk.

My parents are paying
you to make sure I don't off myself too
The school counselor wants reports back.

I'm not interested in offing myself
I just wanna know why.

But I am scared to ask.

After all, no one really knows,
except you, Emily.

So tell me about Emily, you say one day
as the autumn sunlight fades around your office.

She was cool. She liked art and coffee.
She had this disease, something mental I think,
and she didn't like taking meds for it.
She said it dried her up...her artistic nature.

She wore all these funky clothes from thrift stores in
Lakeview. We would shop together. I got this mood ring
on one of our trips. I hold it up. The blackish-blue has
an eerie glow.

Did Emily ever make you any art?

I have a couple of colored pencil drawings and a few
of her poems...but nothing significant.
They took that away...her parents.

I have a sort of assignment for you, you say.
You like to write? You smile.

Ok.

I want you to write a poem for Emily.
It can be any style any topic...just walk around
think about her and then write.

You hand me a pink composition notebook.
This can be your journal.

Ok. I take it shyly.

Out of your office, I am on my way.
And you want me to think about her,
every waking breath. I can't stop thinking
about her death, her last moments on earth,
her last breath.

So I decide to write a poem about all the things
Emily is missing, not being here.

There's a cafe called Kofi
up in Andersonville
They serve organic juices.

I order an apple ginger carrot mint juice.
I see a sign that talks about poets
reading their work.

I am too afraid to read my pithy poems
here but you, Emily, could...
if you were here.

Sitting by Lake Michigan
thinking, scratching the surface
with my pen what lies underneath
the depths of despair

How could God create you to suffer so much?

Is it angst or am I falling where you fell?

I ask myself the questions, the questions
without answers.

The answers come in the form
of more questions.

You are right.
Writing this poem thing,
even if it is indirectly about her,
helps me sort things out.

I no longer want to write
long angsty rants about despair
I want to write with meaning.

I walk through the halls of school
constantly writing in the book
you gave me.

I talk to no one, except in class.
We, Emily and I, hated algebra
and used to compose limericks
about Mr. Q in our notebooks.

I love chemistry and English
but these days I pass those periods
in the poetic zone of my journal.

What are you missing, my friend?
My first A+ on that algebra test
I made high school news team
and will report for our school for
WGN
Ms. Molly says I would be a good
editor-in-chief next year
Your painting won first place in the art contest
I guess some things are worth more when you're dead
The city sparkles with autumn bustle
I bought a Northwestern University t-shirt
and ate at the Weiner Circle our favorite veggie burger
after school the other day—on my way to baby sit the
Morgans.
I sat and wrote at the picnic table in front of the hot dog stand
pretending to have a conversation with you, Emily, in this
journal.

This year we would have swooned over boys, gone
to school semi-formals, gotten our learner's permits,
picked out dresses, taken the PSATs...
I still don't know what I'm living for.

In your office, you ask me how the writing goes
It's okay but it is more like journal entries
You say, Sometimes that makes the best poetry.

We talk about not displacing my grief onto
other things and running around frantically
trying to compensate for what's missing.

What's missing?

Let's see:

a friend to confide in while

sitting on North Avenue Beach our naked feet in the lake;

someone to gallery walk with in Wicker Park
and pretend we are hipster rebels in blue jeans and Doc
Martins.

racing you to read the latest novel at the public library

That's all I can think of for now.

I like to run around the track really fast
track is fun in my gym shorts and sneakers

When I run, I feel free, like a weight has lifted,
I feel you there behind me yet I can forget
your memory.

I can see myself far into the future
and you are only a memory...
I am healed.

But not yet...Not until I make sense
of my guilt, you say.

I still feel like I could have stopped you
and you'd be here today...suppose
I'll always feel that.

You say time heals this.

You ask me if I talk to God.
Yes, I pray.
I guess so, I mean.
I'm sort of agnostic.

You say, talk to Emily like
I would talk to God...
Ask her why and listen
deeply to my heart for the answer.

My head...My heart...
What's the difference?
I suppose I can't begin to do this
until I'm thirty.

There's something about death
that deepens you, it leaves
its empty space above your heart center
and swallows your brain into its perseverating
vortex. One can't escape.
I think it happens to everyone.

Suicide compounds this
Not only are you left with Guilt
but all of a sudden you feel alone
in the world, you know we all die alone
in a world of free will.

I wax philosophic in my journal
My dad says there is no room
for philosophers, they are a luxury
of post-modern society. My dad teaches
at the University of Chicago.
I say sometimes one needs
to play the philosopher in order
to understand and work through pain.
That's what you told me as I prattle
about the minutia of the day.

I have to rehearse for public speaking
class...write a short essay and read
it aloud until I breathe it, memorize it,
feel it and can act it out.
I always thought I was an actress.
I suppose we all are in this thing called life.
Some of us can handle it better than others, you say.

SEPTEMBER DAY
ON THE SHORE WITH THE FAM

The parentals make us all go to the lakeshore
on Sundays. It was a beautiful day to rollerblade
there but I am a bit too old to be seen with the Fam.

I bring this journal and play with space

how   words   look   on   the   page.
I am not sure what I am doing
dabbling in this medium
I was born to write but
as a journalist—I am stymied by poetry.
I feel I am writing journalicious rants.

Self-indulgent is what my parents call it.
So I minimize what I am writing in their presence.
I once showed my mother a poem of mine
and all she said was "That's nice, hon."
Parents just never understand
when you feel greatness coming on.

Greatness. I'm not great. I can't be?

Am I?

I'm one small human
dealing with a great tragedy,
a wasted life.

How can you make sure
her life wasn't a waste?

Hmmm.

You can make sure
you live your life to the
fullest, you say.

What?

Live deeply.

Breathe.

Really see.

and examine your life.

But your words
are short-lived.

I fall victim to blank stares
and frozen smiles
empty echoes from
magazine-heads on the train.

Last night,

I had a dream
You, Emily, were there

but you weren't.

You called for me
You wanted to tell me
something.

I could not make it out.

I woke up.

It's an awful dream
It keeps recurring
every night

Each time, I reach out
to her and she is
so quiet
in a whisper
she is gone.

I can not hear you

or You.

WHAT DO YOU WANT?

FATHER'S DAY

He stands in my doorway

as I type at my laptop

on my bed

Brooklyn, are you alright?

Why, dad?

You left the table really abruptly

I have a lot of work to do

If you ever want to talk about it, I am here.

He turned to go.

Wait! Dad.

Do you know why she did it?

Awe Brooklyn, you can't answer that

with your therapist?

It's just one of those nasty rhetorical questions

Got to talk in his language.

I suppose none of us will ever know til we reach the

great place, he said.

She was sick. She didn't take her meds, he continued.

I am not asking you to understand this all now. Someday, it will gel.

Dad, I love you.

Brooklyn, I love you too.

DREAM SEQUENCE #2

I dream in blue
black and grays.

I awake to a cold,
dark, bedroom.

I am alive.

I am an i.

What to do now?

I am learning
when to use punctuation
and CAPITALIZATION and
when NOT to.

you are a mystery
my mystery
to solve like
Sherlock Holmes or
Harriet the Spy or Nancy Drew or CSI.

The dreams repeat
a living cycle
each time I close my eyes.

A Shadow. A Ghost.

A doppleganger.

A LIE.

I snap awake in your office.
A lie, you say.
She is pulling you under.
You do not deserve this.
You have a life to lead.

Guilt.

And how to move past it?
Another night, another dream,
another nightmare
I tolerate ambiguity and frustration
quite well

you try to reach me
and I can't hear

Maybe, my mother was
right.

Maybe, people who do that
really are in limbo

Limbo must be awful.

I ask you, How do I
make the dreams stop?

Just let go, you say.

Stymied.

I'm not ready
to let go
I need to get a grip,
I want closure.

I doubt
I'll ever get it.

The day
I choose to
show you
my journal
comes with a surprise.

Brooklyn, these are really
good...You have a lot of talent.

Thanks.

You are brave to share
them with me
I hope
this medium helps you
as you go through life
not just in dealing
with your friend's death.

EMILY'S LAST DAY

I'm awake late at night
trying to figure out
her last day, where
her footsteps took her,
what she felt,
what could have set her off
to take the final act.

She wasn't hated at school
but she wasn't popular either.

How does one get that

                hopeless?

The last time

        I saw her
we crossed at her locker
she seemed so

insanely happy

She was grinning
and talking a mile a minute
about going to a street festival
and winning an art prize.

What went wrong?

Emily had a disease,
you say.

It wasn't her fault
and it isn't
        yours
                either.

I hate that disease.

DREAM REQUIEM REVEALED

I know why I keep
having those dreams

you want me to memorialize
your memory
        something concrete
something real

It won't bring you back
It's really for me
so I can have closure
let go and move on

Even though, I cannot
hear you
I feel your words, your pain,
I listen to you with my heart.

She'll always be the best poet,
a great artist,
a funky dresser,
and a freaky cool friend.

I think I'll research
suicide and produce a feature
for Student News

I think it's important...
it's the least I can do.

Why
do people shun
the subject?

is it embarrassing?

Silence kills.

LIVING WITH THE PAIN

I'll carry this pain with me
every day
but what can I do with it?

Turn the pain into a cause
you believe in, turn it into poetry,
turn it into living your best life
and being really present for it, you say.

But what is my best life? Is it
like a personal best?

It is anything and everything you do
to stay healthy and positive about life.

So it's writing and running and photography and
doing student journalism and...
giving it my all.

You got it.

FOCUS ON LIVING

You hand me a flyer
one afternoon
you saw at a local coffee shop.

It's for a poetry group of sorts

They meet at Peet's in Evanston
near Northwestern

You say, I am good enough
to read my work aloud,
to meet people,
to make friends.

You deserve it!
Believe in yourself.

Breathe.

in...out...in...out...

sigh

Maybe, it's time I try...
branch out,
find my group,
a place I belong.

Maybe, it will replace
the emptiness, the hurt.

Nothing will replace her...

ever...

It will be nice to have some
new friends,
I have college to look forward to.

You tell me about
the University of Iowa's
poetry program...

It's a real possibility...

in the running with Northwestern.

Options.

Gotta have options.

A LITTLE BRAVERY IN MY BOWL

My poetry isn't perfect
yet but the more I write
it gets better, I get better
at saying what I need to say

My poetry is like graffiti
written on my soul

I sit in Lincoln Park
on a bench near the zoo
scribbling

Lately, that's what I do

In the yearbook, they'll call
me "the scribbler"

I'm in a funny phase.

Write about a time
when you felt lonely, you told me.

NOW!

I'm in our SUV
My dad is driving me
up to Evanston
to Peet's Coffee shop.

I wonder what the people
will be like.

Will they be feral people
with purple hair and trench coats
and combat boots with one hundred
tattoos and piercings?

I'd be the normal one then,
the one that can fit into any crowd
because I'm bland.

No personality. No style.
Truly objective.

I'm scared.

I might have to peek at
the group and hang out in
the bathroom until my dad comes
back for me.

I like bathrooms.
In junior high, I ate lunch in there.
That's how I met Emily. We
were both in there.

Nerd girls. Word girls.
The art crowd.
the ones who displayed difference

It was
a difference like no other
We weren't retarded, gay, or
fat.

We just were

the kids that spoke their minds
without a care in the world

You, a Girl Kurt Cobain lookalike
So talented yet so
tormented and rash.

So now,

I am alone here
standing in front of Peet's
wondering
whether to go in
clutching my notebook
tightly in my hand.

Breathe. sigh
I open the glass door
and walk in.

In a corner of the room
with some tables pulled together
and chairs all around them

and a small podium in front,
is a group reading from sheets of paper
or small booklets.

I don't have a chapbook yet
and just about everyone here
does or is published in some way
So I sit in the back, listening and taking
notes.

The notes they read
rhyme like jazz piano riffs
even if they aren't written to rhyme

Everyone has this musicality
about their presence

I long for this

I long for peace
from the guilt,
from the nagging self doubt,
from my inner critic

It never comes
suppose it is a permanent condition

I write
the way I talk
and I say
it like it is

tell it like it is
speak what no one wants to hear.

People use vast images
of nature in their poems
while my simple scrawled
lines just seem to talk
about hurt and pain.

These are
happy people
some are my age
most are a bit older,
college maybe.

I talk to no one
and try to blend
into the greenish color
of the walls.

I bend over my notebook
listening
and scribbling

Notes to Self
how to write perfect poetry
stop using i
use more images to describe place and feelings,
metaphors something we learn in English class
learn about different poets people keep quoting:
bishop, kerouac, keats, poe

go to the library and immerse self in the poetry
section
stop being so hyper-critical, which is something
you would tell me

When I meet with you again,
and tell you about it
You say for me to find someone up there
I like and ask them to mentor me.

This seems a little forward
and kind of lame
maybe, once I get to know
the group I can try,
maybe even read something
out loud for the first time.

Do it when you're ready, you say.

I smile.

I wish
I owned all the poets
they have in our library

I'd start a collection--
that I could take on to college with me
and off to explore the world
with

So many different kinds
poetry to break open the hearts

of the world,
poetry to describe a simple moment
food poetry
love poetry, would love to know more about this one
then, there's the depressed poets club filled with names
like sylvia plath and anne sexton and robert lowell,
maybe, that's where my stuff fits right now.

But I don't
want to be like
this forever.

You say, it doesn't have to be that way.

a poem

is playing

with the stylistics

of a moment

describing

the core truth

unraveling emotions

into beauty and image.

I find out today
that those few lines
I submitted in English
class won a prize
and will be published
in our school literary
magazine.

Still,

I worry my writing
still sucks.

I am
the tiny period on the page
forever stopping
with uncertainty.

I am like a phoenix
forever rising
out of the ash
of sadness and grief
to channel
something new, though
I have little clue what that is yet.

my handwriting is chicken-scratch
but I've noticed some kids' have writing
that looks like it belongs in an artist's book.

You say that everyone is an artist
it just depends on where you are coming from.

I give myself
permission
to create something

from nothing

I am a writer.
I write this on my bedroom
mirror in red cursive lipstick.

I take the train to Evanston
walk to Peets,
stand outside the building
for two minutes, then
walk in confidently.

I will talk to someone
there, I will read my work
I will...I will...

I eye this red headed boy
who is kind of cute
My body makes a beeline
for him

Hi, What's your name?
he turns toward me.
All eyes look at me.

I'm Brooklyn.

Oh, I'm Kaplan.

Do you want to sit down
near us tonight? He points to a co-ed bunch
of kids my age.

I take my seat.

Tonight, I hear him say
that the poetry is weak
like coffee watered over with milk
the way I like coffee.

Good strong poetry
is what we want
meaning

Would you like to read,
Brooklyn? Kaplan asked.

Adrenline rushes through me.
Do I run or do I read?

Sure, I guess, I would love to.

I walk slowly to the podium
and open a page in my journal

In a soft voice, I speak:

Sunset fades on the city skyline
My toes touch the cold water of the lake
Alone...I am
And alone we all are
My silhouette dances upon the skyline
as I spin in circles
I must find a way to celebrate your life.

SOMETHING LIKE A BREAKTHROUGH

I'm learning that
I'm good at this,
speaking aloud and
I'm making friends too.

Making friends with myself
and others, just put yourself
out there and you'll be surprised
how many people think like you,
have experienced what you experience.

Kaplan likes me
He says like him, that I'm an existentialist.
I had to look that one up.

It means to deny the existence
of objective values, stressing instead
the reality of human freedoms,
according to the dictionary.

Kaplan forces me to think
and analyze my thoughts
He gives me books to read
He's my age but reads stuff
far advanced for our age.
I don't always understand it
and have to look things up on wikipedia.
I friended Kaplan on Facebook
and I read his blog about

his daily adventures in philosophy.
He goes to a school for gifted kids
and takes college classes.

Kaplan and I have
this kinetic energy
when we are together.
So far, I only see him at
the groups.

You tell me to take it slow.
You also say that our time
is drawing to a close, our
last session is next Monday,
that I am ready to do this
on my own.

I agree. But I'll miss this.
I'll miss spilling my guts to you.
Writing will replace this.

Wish you were here, Emily
So we could discuss Kaplan.

But I know we'll meet
again someday

Our school news team
approved my script
on the suicide segment

and the news editor
wants me to anchor it.

My mother took me shopping
for a new dress to wear
on camera.

I hope this helps
my college application...
but I now cannot decide
between applying to
Northwestern, University of Iowa,
or Evergreen State College
in Washington state--where Kaplan
wants to go. You get to design your own major
there. Junior year will be real important.

Study poetry
or journalism?

Or minor in one and major in the other?

Kaplan and I sit
drinking tall cups of cinnamon
coffee at a bakery in Lincoln Square
not far from where Kaplan's family lives.

I like who I am becoming,
growing into
myself is part of growing up.
I smile to myself
while looking at Kaplan.
Kaplan says that he wants

to take a road trip
to this organic farm
down in Missouri called Dancing Rabbit
where you work and stay for a week.
He heard about it on National Public Radio.
My parents will drive us.
Ask your parents if you can come.

Can I go? Please.

I'll write a story for the newspaper
or a script for the television about
my experience.

Do you know about organic food and farming?
Why don't you do some research on
the subject before you go with him? said dad.

My mom is just happy that
Kaplan's parents will be going with us.
She plans to call them to get acquainted.
They are both some type of scientist. I think
they were hippies way back when...

But when Kaplan's grandmother
passes, his parents call off the trip
indefinitely

Kaplan reads me the poem
he read at his grandmother's funeral
He is dark and brooding now
I am torn between

being a friend
and laying off him for awhile,
giving him some space.
I choose to give him some space
as I have projects to work on.

It is Monday
of our final session.
You hand me a folded piece of paper
I tried to write a poem for you, Brooklyn you say.
The poem reads:
Sing Brooklyn Sing
Say Yes to Life and the Living
Breathe deep and
See what you see
feel what you feel
be who you are
Take up interests and passions
and devote fully to them
Be mindful always
Free your mind,
Stretch and Grow.

It's lovely, I say.
Keep it with you
as a reminder that
a great life awaits you.

I am not sure how to spend
Mondays without seeing you
I think it will be the day
I do nothing

but things for myself
like going to coffee shops,
writing in the park, running,
and taking photographs.

My mood ring shines
a clear blue today

What to do with the pain
now?

Funny.

It doesn't hurt as much now.
Now, that I know what to do.
I smile.

I know you are here,
somewhere,
with us

I'll see you again one day
but first, I have things to do.

Things like high school and
college and who knows what's
in store beyond that.

BUMPING IN, BUMPING OUT

I ran into your mom today
in the grocery store while
I was getting our list for my mom.

All tight-lipped, she barely acknowledged me
walking past whispering "Hello, Brooklyn."
pushing her cart quickly.
It might have been a scene
out of *Real Housewives*.

You came in, Emily
and you came out of my life
in a flash
All I have left are the memories
and I can hear your voice fading fast
in my mind.

MOVING ON

springtime

Kaplan called yesterday
asking me to his semi-formal dance
"Do you want to be my girlfriend?"
I'm someone's girlfriend.
Kaplan and I entered a citywide
poetry slam sponsored by the mayor's office
and held at the library.

I have writing to do
I must write seven new poems
for the slam
I will write them about sunshine,
the air in our city, high school ironies,
that kind of stuff. I'm trying to write
more persona poems--taking a stab at comedy.

I take Emily with me
and she becomes part of who I am
as I leave childhood behind.

I take deep inspiration
from our Lake standing
with my toes clutching the sand
water rushing over them;
sunlight melting
my heart.

SLAMMIN' WITH MY KIND

I have a tribe
its made of word people
and I rap and hum and drum
and write my way through
life's disasters.

Kaplan and I,
a cosmic pair,
a team of word lovers
composing poems and lyric essays
for our own chapbook.
It doesn't have a title yet.
But there is something romantic and
revolutionary about the title "untitled."

It has a counterculture rhythm to it.

We are up at the library one night
a week...practicing.

Practicing how to recite poetry.
If you go too slow or too fast or pronounce
the wrong syllables, it takes on another meaning.

Every weekend, we slam in a different coffee shop
getting ready for the Teen Poetry Slam.

In school, I found out my segment on suicide
won a journalism prize. It will look nice on my college apps

but the segment meant so much more.

It meant losing a dear friend who you grew up with,
and losing your childhood ways and adopting new ones.

My kind, my tribe
has hipsters, goths,
poor kids from Bronxville
and the South side, intellectuals, students,
and plain people like me. We
come together to celebrate life, create art,
make word images. Our slam team goes
against other teams throughout the city.

We are a gang, a poem gang, the only good type
A friend at school is going to produce a segment
on us for Student News.

I DREAMT LAST NIGHT...

that your words, Emily,
spoke through me
I woke up
with poems, your poems,
coming so fast and furious

I scribbled one down
but it turned out to be nonsense.

It is as if your words
are a mystery for me
to unravel.

Do I need to go back
to Dr. K?

She would be so disappointed
in me.

Tomorrow, after school,
I'll stop by her office.

NO APPOINTMENT, NO MONEY, NO PROBLEM

I just show up
and you are with a client
You tell me I have to wait
if it is urgent and then you
can give me a half hour.

My thoughts wander
while I wait in you empty
waiting room. I can't concentrate
on your magazines.

Tears run down my face
as I think about Emily.
Why is this happening now?

I am sitting on your couch
Brooklyn, It's okay. There are going
to be days when the tears come back.
Memory is a funny thing.
It sneaks up on you when you least expect it.

What about my dream? I feel I am to unravel
the mystery, her mystery in her poetry?

Here's what you do: Sit very quiet with pen and paper
and listen to her words carefully. Practice the meditation
exercises we discussed to get closer to the dream
consciousness.

After you do this enough times, try letting the poem she speaks go.

Brooklyn, I have a client waiting but if you need an appointment...

Thank you Dr. K. And I ducked out of there.

UNRAVELING YOUR MYSTERY

I sit quietly with a blank journal
in my bedroom
I have dedicated to solving this
Poet Detective--a Literary Nancy Drew
I can do this
The depression is gone now
I can see life now and I have one.
But I have unfinished business
your business.

Calm, silent, calm

Thoughts start to blur

My thoughts.

thoughts...just thoughts

I am waiting

Emily, can you hear me?

Are the tears just a bad day, a bad mood?
Will this happen from time to time, like Dr. K said?

God, if you are there, this really is a crazy, tragic,
magic life.

Wait I don't believe in God yet!

But I believe in Emily and her poetry and her mystery.

Speak to me. Speak.

Maybe, I need to visit her grave.

ABOUT AS GOTH AS YOU GET

I lean against your grave
with my notebook listening
to the Chicago wind

The cemetery is high upon a hill
with some ancient stones

I will stay until it gets dark and maybe
your ghost will come out and talk to me

Kaplan wanted to have a seance complete
with a ouija board but

I think that is lame.

I just need to be alone with you and the wind.

YOU ENTER ME

My thoughts
spin with your thoughts
gentle breezes and untouched saplings
With time, they get louder
Louder LOUDER

Out of the insanity, I hear you:

Brooklyn, It's me, Emmie
Write my words and speak them loud

I live elsewhere now, on another plain,
My mind was too fragile for this earth
I saw too many connections unraveling
in the universe
I wanted to do them all, gather them all
tie them in a knot and save them
but they grew too fast and too loud
so I had to kill them, i smashed them
into tiny shatterings
they sprinkled all over the earth

My words are yours now
It is up to you
to pick up the pieces
one by one and solve the puzzle
Each word completes the poem.

Emily, where are you?
She was gone and the graveyard
fell silent.

I looked up from my notebook
to see Kaplan a few feet away
What are you doing here?

You told me this is where you go sometimes
to write. When you weren't at your house or the
coffee shop, I came here.

Oh, Kaplan. I fall into his arms
like such a dumb damzel.

He kisses me; I kiss him
I don't know which happened
first.

It just felt right then and there.

We wrestled on the grass
with our clothes between our virginity

Naked. We made love
her headstone as witness.

LOSS, LOST, LOSER

I can't believe it is lost.
This loss is of another kind.

This time, I feel I am on the beginning of something
not watching its end.

I still feel like such a loser for not waiting
'til marriage
but so what if it doesn't last

Kaplan, is here now.

At least, he used a condom.

The great poet Oscar Wilde once said,
"Tis better to have loved and lost then never
loved at all."

I'll have many great romances in my life before
I find the one.

No one at school knows that I wear the scarlet A.

Hey, great poets have to be different.
Think. Write. Be.

Different.

MY LIFE UNTITLED

I have this mystery
I have to solve
and I lost my flower

stress

Keeping these secrets
from everyone
how crazy life has become

Your voice
sticks in my head

This makes no sense.

Her voice in my head,
deciphering her poetry.

Am I going crazy
or is this residual grief?

Grief has many forms:
some hide in activity,
some sink into depression,
some never fill the pit of loneliness,
some need people all the time,
some just become uhhh crazy.

NEED YOU NOW

I walked all the way to your parents
home

I need to see your journals, diaries,
books of poems floating around your
untouched room

I need some answers only they can
provide.

I ring the doorbell awkwardly
Her mother answers
"Hello, Brooklyn, Come on in.
Have a cup of tea and a snack."

She seems to be beginning to move past
the grief fog--if one ever does?

I tell her I've got a dilemma
compelling me to solve Emily's
mystery.

Sound sane, please.

I need to look through her room
I need one last glimpse into what it
looked like.

"Well, I don't like people rummaging
up there, upsetting things. I need to preserve it."

She sighs.

"But I suppose for you, since the two of you
were close, go on up. Put everything back the way
you found it."

ALONE AMONGST YOUR THINGS

Your room—lonely and dusty
a mausoleum of a young artist
who failed at trying
trying to fight a disease

Your awards for swimming,
your laptop which got us in trouble
for spamming the mean girls,
shelves and shelves of books and journals,
your easel, boxes of unsent letters to
boys you liked, a closet full of artist smocks
and thrift store specials.

I find your book of poems bound in black canvas.

Open a page

i write these lines
someday when i'm not around
i can't live with these pills
side effects are worse than the disease
All those who follow me
follow your heart
and you will do me justice.

Follow your heart, an interesting line
Am I following my heart?
Journalism. Poetry. Science.

Where does my heart lie?

Poem Poem Poem.

A GANG CALLED POETRY

We have this gang
We fight other gangs
not with bullets
but with words

We write and
we face off in libraries,
coffeehouses, community centers

Our gang wears all black with purple
bandana armbands
Kaplan says the purple makes the guys
look like fags
But we let a fourteen-year-old girl, our youngest
member, choose our color

Slammin'

is my life

My life consists of Kaplan, poetry gang, slams,
and school

i'm hardly at home or alone on my own

Kaplan and I spend a lot more time since we had sex

We haven't done it again

We're both frightened by our own power.

72

TEENAGE SEX

What is the difference

between

sex

and

love?

Is

sex

right

if

love

is uncertain or cannot last?

SLAMMIN' TIME

synesthesia
surrounds the city
it is my job
to show you this
like you were a tourist

high pitch screams
waling, clunks of
the city trains
high above

This one goes out to
the beaches sprawling
up the coast of our lake,
the high rises condos popping up
like vertical ice cube trays,
the Carl Sandburg apartments to
Cabrini Green to two flats in Lincoln Park
and Rogers Park

to the Jews, to the blacks, to the Irish, to
Hispanics, to all its varied ethnicities

to Northwestern, to DePaul, to Columbia College,
to U of Chicago

Words etch themselves around us
petroglyphs: the code to our time

simple signs with directions
oxymorons

We've learned words
to build a word toolbox
for our rhymes and limes
and phrases probably worth a dime

WE WON!

We won the state slam at the Daley Center!
onto nationals in San Francisco

GOING TO THE FRISCO BAY

Our little gang is going to Frisco
Kaplan tells me there is this cool
bookstore there City Light Books
that was founded by the Beats

Frisco is the stomping ground of
Jack Kerouac

It is the home of artists and writers
an old city
where poetry sings off the palm trees

I get to see another city.

But first I must stop these dreams
from coming back

I must be sane

If part of me never let you go,
then I must do it now.

FEARLESS

I let go

of the beautiful and terrible

things in this world

My poetry

grounds me

Through the pain,

I find my truth.

I am fearless.

The City has dangers,

the unknown, places

in the future, the me

I don't know yet.

People say,

Without G-D

there is no protection

from evil.

Since I don't believe

like that,

Poetry is my G-D.

Maybe someday,

my conception

of HIM will change.

GETTING READY FOR THE NATIONAL SLAM

I want to stand on the Golden Gate Bridge,
go to City Lights Books,
visit teahouses, shop in vintage stores,
see Haight Ashbury,
I want to see where progressive ideas
fly off trees.

We are writing the

                        perfect poem

then rehearsing it to its death

There will be gangs--one from every state
all who want to be champions

We may not win but we will have fun

and see San Francisco

I wish you were here, Emily

Wish you could see who I am becoming.

FRISCO POETRY

Our first day out here

we visit a Japanese tea garden

beautiful silences

as we meditate between the plants

We rehearse our poems in a big hall

at the Holiday Inn on the city's outskirts

Soon we will converge upon an auditorium

at San Francisco State University

to give it our all.

Coffee and vegan food sustains us.

After the competition, we will be tourists.

For now, Kaplan and I must practice

our duet poem and a bunch of others

we will perform on our own.

SLAMMIN' IN CISCO

This feels like college

getting up and reading out loud

on stage.

Dr. K would be so proud of me.

I've come a long way in a year.

There are poets here dressed in artist garb,
military wannabes, Che Guerra fanatics

It's intimidating.

But a couple of deep breaths and we don't let it

get to us.

Anyhow, I can't tell who they want to be

I'm glad I'm plain old preppie me.

My last poem I read to the judges

is one for you, Emily.

Can it be so much I learned
from your death?

I packed my iPod
with music you and I liked
lessons learned from its soul
from yours to mine
You're here
everywhere
with me.

UNDERNEATH THE BRIDGE

We are patting each other

on the back and tears slip down

tears of frustration

Maybe, next year

Poetry is something you grow into

as you grow into yourself, who you

are going to be.

Don't worry, I know I still have talent

at this.

We are strong. We will carry on becomes

our motto.

Later, Kaplan and I take a cab

to the Golden Gate Bridge

so I can take a picture.

Walking along the sidewalk

with vehicles passing by,

Kaplan spots something in the distance.

TAKING THE LEAP

Be Brave, Brooklyn

Don't have a panic attack now.

We get closer to the middle of the bridge

and we see someone perched on the ledge

What should we do? Call the Cops said Kaplan.

No, let me handle this.

I can't watch this happen again

Someone else going through what I go through

for Emily

I shout up to the girl on the ledge

holding on for dear life

You don't have to do this, you know

Life gets better if you let it.

You don't have my life, she shouted back.

My friend killed herself, I yell.

I live with her pain every day.

It's not pretty. It's not fun.

But I deal.

The girl said, My parents are dead, my brother is on the streets,

my life is not worth living.

You will find happiness if you look inside yourself, I say.

Really? said the girl.

You mean my problems will someday go away?

Problems come and go.

Just force yourself to live in the present tense.

The girl slowly alights toward the sidewalk.

When she reaches the bottom,

She approaches me and puts out her hand.

We shake.

Thank you she says. I was ready to jump today.

But maybe, I'll try living like you do instead.

She turns and walks away.

As she fades into the distance,

Kaplan turns to me and says Wow.

You saved her, man.

Maybe for the moment, I say, We'll see.

The sunset fades as we head to a coffee shop

I look straight ahead of me at the city's peoples

against the urban backdrop.

And I smile...

because I have found myself

and I am at peace.

Author's Note

I lost my best friend to suicide at age 37. I was devastated. I wrote this novella to show that you can recover from the grief that follows.

If you have mental health problems or know someone who does, please check out the following resources.

Active Minds: www.activeminds.org
NAMI: www.nami.org
DBSA: www.dbsalliance.org
The Talk: 1-800-273-TALK

Acknowledgments

I'd like to thank the following people who made this production possible: Cheryl Cranick for all her help with the redesign; and my father Alan Maislen for his support and editing. To my husband, Robert, and his Monday Night Wrestling, which gave me the time to write this, you have been the shining light in my life. And, of course, to Cat, who we lost too soon, and who taught me about light, laughter, and strength.